WITHDRAWN

THE PIG IS IN THE PANTRY,

THE CAT IS ON THE SHELF

by **Shirley Mozelle**   Illustrated by **Jennifer Plecas**

Clarion Books • New York

Clarion Books
a Houghton Mifflin Company imprint
215 Park Avenue South, New York, NY 10003
Text copyright © 2000 by Shirley Mozelle
Illustrations copyright © 2000 by Jennifer Plecas

The illustrations for this book were executed in pen and ink and watercolor.
The type for this book was set in 17-point Esprit.

Printed in Singapore.

Library of Congress Cataloging-in-Publication Data

Mozelle, Shirley.
The pig is in the pantry, the cat is on the shelf / by Shirley Mozelle ;
illustrated by Jennifer Plecas.
p.   cm.
Summary: Having left his house unlocked to go shopping, Mr. McDuffel returns to find
that the barnyard animals have taken it over and created chaos.
ISBN 0-395-78627-4
[1. Domestic animals—Fiction.] I. Plecas, Jennifer, ill.
II. Title.
PZ7. M868Co   1997
[E]—dc20   96-30212
CIP
AC

TWP   10   9   8   7   6   5   4   3   2   1

For Jennifer Greene and Nina Ignatowicz
—S. M.

THE CLOCK STRIKES EIGHT.

Mr. McDuffel leaves for town
to buy a bag of flour.
In a hurry, he forgets to lock the door.

"Let's go inside," says the cow.
"Oink!" says the pig.
"Ehhhhhh!" says the goat.
"Kakakakaaa!" says the hen.
"Nayyyyyy!" says the horse.
"Baaaaaa!" says the ewe.
"Quack!" says the duck.
And the goose on the roof says, *"Honk! Honk!"*

In they go.
One, two, three, four, five, six, seven.
The goose makes *eight*.

6

Mr. McDuffel's cat hisses and arches her back.

Now the cow is in the kitchen
and the pig is in the pantry.

The goat is in the tub
and the hen is on the bed.

The horse is on the sofa
and the ewe is on the rug.

The duck is on the table . . . and the goose—
silly, silly goose—is making faces in the mirror.

9

THE
CLOCK
STRIKES
NINE.

Mr. McDuffel's truck hits a bump.
POP! Ssssshhh! goes the tire.

"Let's dress up!" says the cow.
The cow puts on a hat and the pig puts on a tie.
The goat puts on a shirt and the hen puts on a sock.
The horse puts on a scarf and the ewe puts on a shoe.
The duck puts on a watch . . .
and the goose—happy, happy, silly goose—
puts on the radio.
Two. Four. Six. Eight.
They dance around the house.
The cat jumps to the mantel.

12

"Quackle-dackle!"

"Honkle-donkle! Honk! Honk! Honk!"

15

THE CLOCK STRIKES TWELVE.

Mr. McDuffel is on the road again.
Putt! Putt! Varoooooom!

"Let's eat!" says the cow.
The cow sets the table
and the pig bakes biscuits.
The goat swirls spaghetti
and the hen pours juice.

17

The horse sweeps crumbs
and the ewe washes dishes.
The duck cleans the table . . .
and the goose—
full-to-the-bill, happy, happy, silly goose—
stretches out on pillows and watches TV.

The cat climbs to a high shelf.

At four Mr. McDuffel walks through the door.
"Out! Out! Out!"

He runs, he chases, he catches, and he places.
The cat purrs.

TICK-
TOCK.
THE
CLOCK
STRIKES
FIVE.

The cow, the pig, the goat, the hen, the duck,
the horse, and the ewe are in the barnyard.
And the goose—
silly, silly, happy, curious goose—
is in a dither,
chasing bugs above her head.

THE CLOCK STRIKES SIX.

Mops, rags, buckets, and brooms.
Mr. McDuffel is cleaning, straightening, mending, and fixing.

The cat laps milk.

Bath time.
Quiet time.

THE CLOCK STRIKES NINE.

The moon is high in the sky
and the night is bright.
Mr. McDuffel is very tired
and settles in his bed.
The cat snuggles atop his head.

29

Inside the barn
the cow, the pig, the goat, the hen, the duck,
the horse, and the ewe are asleep . . .

but the goose—
curious, curious, happy, silly goose—
is in a panic.
WHOOOOOOSH! She is on her back.

Outside,
a skunk, an opossum, an owl, a raccoon—
and a spooky, spooky bat—
are looking into the bag of flour
Mr. McDuffel left in his truck.